PUPPY!

keith graves

A NEAL PORTER BOOK
ROARING BROOK PRESS
NEW YORK

Copyright © 2016 by Keith Graves

A Neal Porter Book

Published by Roaring Brook Press

Roaring Brook Press is a division of Holtzbrinck Publishing Holdings Limited Partnership

175 Fifth Avenue, New York, New York 10010

The artwork in this book was created using pencil and digital color.

mackids.com

Library of Congress Cataloging-in-Publication Data

Graves, Keith, author, illustrator.

Puppy! / Keith Graves. – First edition.

pages cm

"A Neal Porter book."

Summary: "When a cave boy gets a 'puppy,' things don't quite turn out as he expected"– Provided by publisher.

ISBN 978-1-62672-225-5 (hardback)

[1. Prehistoric peoples–Fiction. 2. Prehistoric animals–Fiction. 3. Dogs–Fiction. 4. Pets–Fiction. 5. Humorous stories.] I. Title.

PZ7.G77524Pu 2016

[E]–dc23

2015008413

Roaring Brook Press books may be purchased for business or promotional use. For information on bulk purchases please contact Macmillan Corporate and Premium Sales Department at (800) 221-7945 x5442 or by email at specialmarkets@macmillan.com.

First edition 2016

Printed in China by RR Donnelley Asia Printing Solutions Ltd., Dongguan City, Guangdong Province

1 3 5 7 9 10 8 6 4 2

For Rusty, greatest puppy of them all

Cave boy Trog
had all the best toys.

A stick.

A rock.

Mud.

But Trog did not want
a stick, a rock, or mud.

Trog wanted a . . .

Trog brought his new friend home.

Trog introduced the puppy to his family.

Suddenly the puppy began to cry.

Boo hoooooo!

Then it ate the sofa.

Munch
Munch
Munch

The puppy cried at bedtime.

Then the puppy cried and ate the bed.

Trog tried
everything
to cheer the
puppy up.

He gave the
puppy a bath,

took the puppy
for a walk,

and scratched the
puppy's belly.

Nothing worked.

Then Trog's family had a new visitor.

When Trog opened his eyes, the giant visitor was gone.
So was the puppy.

Trog found them at the edge of the swamp.

Then Trog noticed something. The puppy was not crying. The puppy was happy.

The puppy was home.

Trog missed
the puppy.

He found a new stick,

a new rock,

and something even
better than mud.